The Fearless Shark
El Tiburón Sin Miedo

D1360717

无畏的 鲨鱼
두려움 없는

Explore Animals and Opposites in English, Spanish, Chinese & Korean

ISBN: 978-1-949676-06-8
David Ming
Copyright © 2019 by David Yeh
Yeh! Books, a division of Yeh! Made
Everyday Concepts Vol. 3

Amazon 812 95 9/19

DL E MIN 200549

Melissa Public Library
Melissa, Texas

YM

The fearless shark hunts beneath the waves.
El tiburón sin miedo caza bajo las olas.

无畏的 鲨鱼 在 海浪 下 觅食。
WúWèiDe ShāYú Zài HǎiLàng Xià MìShí.
無畏的 鯊魚 在 海浪 下 覓食。

두려움 없는 상어가 파도 아래서 먹이를 찾고 있어요.
Duryeoum eomneun sangeoga pado araeseo meogireul chatgo isseoyo.

The shy condor soars above the mountains.
El cóndor tímido se eleva sobre las montañas.

害羞的　禿鹰　在　高山　上　飞翔。
HàiXiūDe　TūYīng　Zài　GāoShān Shàng FēiXiáng.
害羞的　禿鷹　在　高山　上　飛翔。

수줍은　콘드로가　산위로　솟아　올라요.
Sujubeun　kondeuroga　sanwiro　sosa　ollayo.

The noisy rooster guards the farm.
El gallo ruidoso vigila la granja.

吵闹的 公鸡 守卫着 农场。
ChǎoNàoDe GōngJī ShǒuWèiZhe NóngChǎng.
吵鬧的 公雞 守衛著 農場。

시끄러운 수탉이 농장을 지키고 있어요.
Sikkeureoun sutalgi nongjangeul jikigo isseoyo

The quiet turtle patrols the swamp.
La tortuga tranquila patrulla el pantano.

安静的 乌龟 在 沼泽 巡逻。
ĀnJìngDe WūGuī Zài ZhǎoZé XúnLuó.
安靜的 烏龜 在 沼澤 巡邏。

조용한 거북이가 늪을 순찰하고 있어요.
Joyonghan geobugiga neupeul sunchalhago isseoyo.

The furry tigers peek their heads out of the cave.
Los tigres peludos asoman sus cabezas fuera de la cueva.

毛茸茸的 老虎 从 洞穴 里 偷看。
MáoRóngRōngDe LǎoHǔ Cóng DòngXué Lǐ Tōu Kàn.
毛茸茸的 老虎 從 洞穴 裡 偷看。

털이 많은 호랑이가 동굴 밖으로 머리를 내밀고 쳐다보아요.
Teori maneun horangiga donggul bakkeuro meorireul naemilgo chyeodaboayo.

The hairless dog barks at the cactus.
El perro calvo le ladra al cactus.

无毛的 小狗 对着 仙人掌 吠叫。
WúMáoDe XiǎoGǒu DuìZhe XiānRénZhǎng FèiJiào.
無毛的 小狗 對著 仙人掌 吠叫。

털이 없는 개가 선인장을 보고 짖어요.
Teori eomneun gaega seoninjangeul bogo jijeoyo.

The smooth stingray relaxes on the seafloor.
La raya suave se relaja en el fondo marino.

平滑的 黄貂鱼 在 海底 放松。
PíngHuáDe HuángDiāoYú Zài HǎiDǐ FàngSōng.
平滑的 黃貂魚 在 海底 放鬆。

매끄러운 가오리가 바다밑에서 편안히 쉬고 있어요.
Maekkeureoun gaoriga badamiteseo pyeonanhi swigo isseoyo.

The spiky sea urchin lies on the beach.
El erizo de mar puntiagudo se encuentra en la playa.

沙滩 上 有 一个 多刺的 海胆。
ShāTān Shàng Yǒu YīGè DuōCìDe HǎiDǎn.
沙灘 上 有 一個 多刺的 海膽。

뾰족한 성게가 해변에 누워 있어요.
Ppyojokan seonggega haebyeone nuwo isseoyo.

The panda bear eats alone.
El oso panda come solo.

熊猫 独自 进食。
XióngMāo DúZì JìnShí.
熊貓 獨自 進食。

판다가 혼자 먹고 있어요.
Pandaga honja meokgo isseoyo.

The ants lift the leaf together.
Las hormigas levantan la hoja juntas.

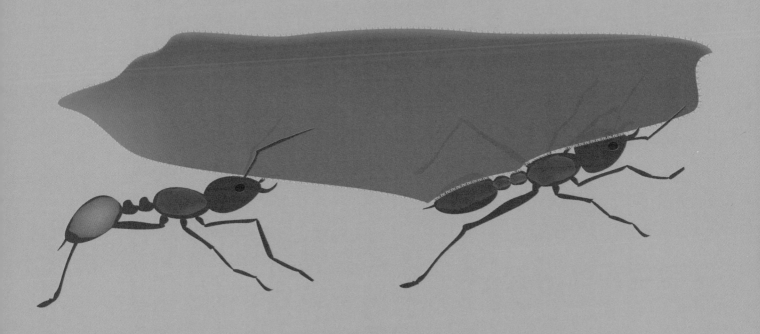

蚂蚁们 一起 将 叶子 抬起。
MǎYǐMen YīQǐ Jiāng YèZi TáiQǐ.
螞蟻們 一起 將 葉子 抬起。

개미들이 함께 잎사귀를 들어올려요.
Gaemideuri hamkke ipsagwireul deureoollyeoyo.

The quick cobra slithers across the desert.
La cobra rápida se desliza a través del desierto.

快速的 眼镜蛇 爬行 沙漠。
KuàiSùDe YǎnJìngShé PáXíng ShāMò.
快速的 眼鏡蛇 爬行 沙漠。

재빠른 코브라가 사막을 스르르 가로지르고 있어요.
Jaeppareun kobeuraga samageul seureureu garojireugo isseoyo.

The slow seahorse lives near the reef.
El caballito de mar lento vive cerca del arrecife.

缓慢的 海马 住 在 礁石 附近。
HuǎnMànDe HǎiMǎ Zhù Zài JiāoShí FùJìn.
緩慢的 海馬 住 在 礁石 附近。

느린 해마는 암초 근처에 살아요.
Neurin haemaneun amcho geuncheoe sarayo.

The lazy crocodile rests on a log.
El cocodrilo perezoso descansa sobre un tronco.

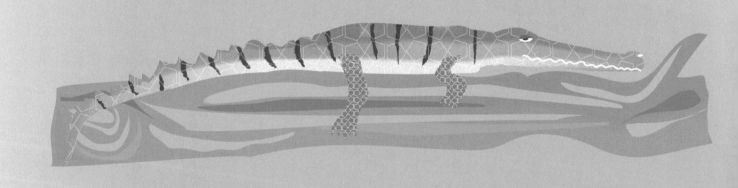

懒惰的 鳄鱼 躺 在 原木 上。
LǎnDuòDe ÈYú Tǎng Zài YuánMù Shàng.
懶惰的 鱷魚 躺 在 原木 上。

게으른 악어가 통나무 위에서 쉬고 있어요.
Geeureun ageoga tongnamu wieseo swigo isseoyo.

The industrious silkworm builds a cocoon.
El gusano de seda trabajador construye un capullo.

勤劳的 蚕宝宝 造了 一个 茧。
QínLáoDe CánBǎoBǎo ZàoLe YīGè Jiǎn.
勤勞的 蠶寶寶 造了 一個 繭。

부지런한 누에가 고치를 만들고 있어요.
Bujireonhan nuega gochireul mandeulgo isseoyo.

The fox is a carnivore.
El zorro es un carnívoro.

狐狸 是个 肉食 动物。
HúLí ShìGè RòuShí DòngWù.
狐狸 是個 肉食 動物。

여우는 육식동물이에요.
Yeouneun yuksikdongmurieyo.

The rabbit is an herbivore.
El conejo es un herbivoro.

兔子 是个 草食 动物。
TùZi ShìGè CǎoShí DòngWù.
兔子 是個 草食 動物。

토끼는 초식동물이에요.
Tokkineun chosikdongmurieyo.

The diurnal reindeer roams the glacier during the day.
El reno diurno deambula por el glaciar durante el día.

昼出的 驯鹿 白天 漫步 冰川。
ZhòuChūDe XùnLù BáiTiān MànBù BīngChuān.

畫出的 馴鹿 白天 漫步 冰川。

주행성 순록이 빙하를 돌아다니고 있어요.
Juhaengseong sullogi binghareul doradanigo isseoyo.

The nocturnal bat stretches its wings at night.
El murciélago nocturno estira su alas por la noche.

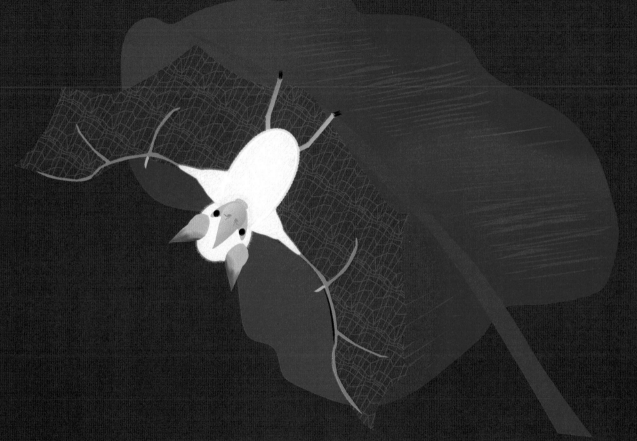

夜行的　蝙蝠　晚上　　伸展　翅膀。
YèXíngDe　BiānFú　WǎnShàng　ShēnZhǎn　ChìBǎng.

夜行的　蝙蝠　晚上　　伸展　翅膀。

야행성　　박쥐가　날개를　펴고　있어요.
Yahaengseong bakiwiga　nalgaereul　pyeogo　isseoyo

The giraffes stand to the left of the pond.
Las jirafas se paran a la izquierda del estanque.

长颈鹿 站 在 池塘 的 左边。
ChángJǐngLù Zhàn Zài ChíTáng De ZuǒBiān.
長頸鹿 站 在 池塘 的 左邊。

기린이 연못 왼쪽에 있어요.
Girini yeonmot oenjjoge isseoyo.

The baby koala bear prefers the right side of the tree.
El oso koala bebé prefiere el lado derecho del árbol.

宝宝 无尾熊 喜欢 在 树 的 右侧。
BǎoBǎo WúWěiXióng XǐHuān Zài Shù De YòuCè.
寶寶 無尾熊 喜歡 在 樹 的 右側。

아기 코알라는 나무 오른쪽을 좋아해요.
Agi koallaneun namu oreunjjogeul joahaeyo.

Melissa Public Library
Melissa, Texas

The big whale sings a lullaby.
La gran ballena canta una canción de cuna.

巨大的　鯨鱼　唱着　一首　摇篮曲。
JùDàDe　JīngYú　ChàngZhe Yī Shǒu　YáoLánQǔ.
巨大的　鯨魚　唱著　一首　搖籃曲。

커다란　고래가　자장가를　불러요.
Keodaran　goraega　jajanggareul　bulleoyo.

The small butterflies dance in the wind.
Las mariposas pequeñas bailan en el viento.

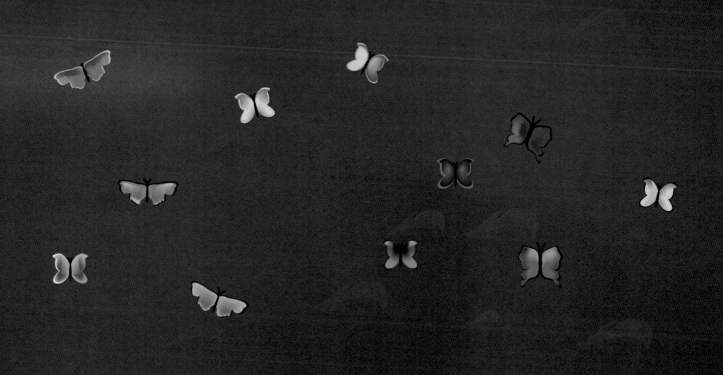

小小的　蝴蝶　在　风　中　起舞。
XiǎoXiǎoDe　HúDié　Zài　Fēng　Zhōng　QǐWǔ.
小小的　蝴蝶　在　風　中　起舞。

작은　나비가　바람에　따라　춤을　추어요.
Jageun　nabiga　barame　ttara　chumeul　chueoyo.

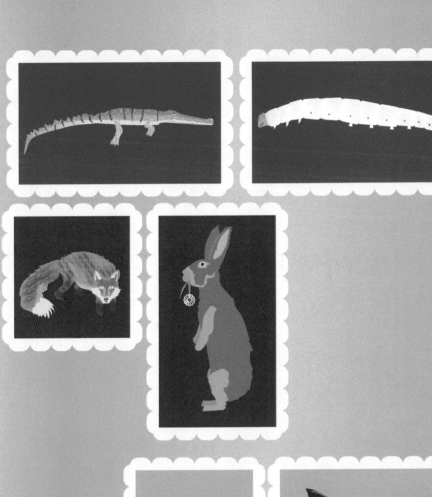

Animals	Animales	动物 / DòngWù / 動物	동물 / Dongmul
		Simplified / Mandarin PīnYīn / Traditional	Korean / Korean Romanization
		简体中文 / 拼音 / 繁體中文	한국어 / 로마자 표기법
Shark	Tiburón	鲨鱼 / ShāYú / 鯊魚	상어 / Sangeo
Condor	Cóndor	秃鹰 / TūYīng / 禿鷹	콘도르 / Kondoreu
Rooster	Gallo	公鸡 / GōngJī / 公雞	수탉 / Sutak
Turtle	Tortuga	乌龟 / WūGuī / 烏龜	거북이 / Geobugi
Tiger	Tigre	老虎 / LǎoHǔ / 老虎	호랑이 / Horangi
Dog	Perro	狗 / Gǒu / 狗	개 / Gae
Stingray	Raya	黄貂鱼 / HuángDiāo Yú / 黃貂魚	가오리 / Gaori
Sea Urchin	Erizo de Mar	海胆 / HǎiDǎn / 海膽	성게 / Seongge
Panda Bear	Oso Panda	熊猫 / XióngMāo / 熊貓	판다 / Panda
Ant	Hormiga	蚂蚁 / MǎYǐ / 螞蟻	개미 / Gaemi
Cobra	Cobra	眼镜蛇 / YǎnJìngShé / 眼鏡蛇	코브라 / Kobeura
Sea Horse	Caballito de Mar	海马 / HǎiMǎ / 海馬	해마 / Haema
Crocodile	Crocodilo	鳄鱼 / ÈYú / 鱷魚	악어 / Ageo
Silkworm	Gusano de Seda	蚕 / Cán / 蠶	누에 / Nue
Fox	Zorro	狐狸 / HúLí / 狐狸	여우 / Yeou
Rabbit	Conejo	兔子 / TùZi / 兔子	토끼 / Tokki
Reindeer	Reno	驯鹿 / XùnLù / 馴鹿	순록 / Sullok
Bat	Murciélago	蝙蝠 / BiānFú / 蝙蝠	박쥐 / Bakjwi
Giraffe	Jirafa	长颈鹿 / ChángJǐngLù / 長頸鹿	기린 / Girin
Koala Bear	Oso Koala	无尾熊 / WúWěiXióng / 無尾熊	코알라 / Koalla
Whale	Ballena	鲸鱼 / JīngYú / 鯨魚	고래 / Gorae
Butterfly	Mariposa	蝴蝶 / HúDié / 蝴蝶	나비 / Nabi

Opposites	Opuestos	正反 / ZhèngFǎn / 正反	반대말 / Bandaemal
		Simplified / Mandarin PīnYīn / Traditional 简体中文 / 拼音 / 繁體中文	Korean / Korean Romanization 한국어 / 로마자 표기법
Beneath	Bajo	底下 / DǐXia / 底下	아래 / Arae
Above	Sobre	上方 / ShàngFāng / 上方	위 / Wi
Loud	Ruidoso	吵闹 / ChǎoNào / 吵鬧	시끄러운 / Sikkeureoun
Quiet	Tranquilo	安静 / ĀnJìng / 安靜	조용한 / Joyonghan
Furry	Peludo	毛茸茸 / MáoRóngRōng / 毛茸茸	털이많은 / Teorimaneun
Hairless	Calvo	无毛 / Wú Máo / 無毛	털이없는 / Teorieomneun
Smooth	Suave	平滑 / PíngHuá / 平滑	매끈한 / Maekkeunhan
Spiky	Puntiagudo	多刺 / DuōCì / 多刺	뾰족한 / Ppyojokan
Alone	Solo	独自 / DúZì / 獨自	혼자 / Honja
Together	Juntos	一起 / YīQǐ / 一起	함께 / Hamkke
Quick	Rápido	快 / Kuài / 快	재빠른 / Jaeppareun
Slow	Lento	慢 / Màn / 慢	느린 / Neurin
Lazy	Perezoso	懒惰 / LǎnDuò / 懶惰	게으른 / Geeureun
Industrious	Trabajador	勤劳 / QínLáo / 勤勞	부지런한 / Bujireonhan
Carnivore	Carnívoro	肉食动物 / RòuShí DòngWù / 肉食動物	육식 동물 / Yugsik Dongmul
Herbivore	Herbívoro	草食动物 / CǎoShí DòngWù / 草食動物	초식 동물 / Chosig Dongmul
Diurnal	Diurno	昼出 / ZhòuChū / 晝出	주행성 / Juhaengseong
Nocturnal	Nocturno	夜行 / YèXíng / 夜行	야행성 / Yahaengseong
Left	Izquierda	左 / Zuǒ / 左	왼쪽 / Oenjjok
Right	Derecho	右 / Yòu / 右	오른쪽 / Oreunjjok
Big	Grande	大 / Dà / 大	큰 / Keun
Small	Pequeño	小 / Xiǎo / 小	작은 / Jageun

a Publ...
Melissa Texas

65977061R00018

Melissa Public Library
Melissa, Texas

Made in the USA
Columbia, SC
15 July 2019